Goodbye Monsters

by Benjamin & Susan Hemme
illustrated by Kenny DeWitt

ISBN-10: 061599704X
ISBN-13: 978-0-615-99704-9

Printed and bound in China

115 Bluebill Drive
Savannah, GA 31419
United States

This book was published with the assistance of the helpful folks at DragonPencil.com

It is with gratitude that we dedicate this book;

To our loving family who has always believed in and supported us.

And to parents everywhere, who have spent countless nights chasing the monsters away.

This is Ben.

Ben is afraid of monsters. Big and tall or short and small.

Ben is afraid of all monsters.

Ben is scared to go
to sleep at night.

He believes that
monsters are living
under his bed and in
his closet.

To help keep the monsters away, he sleeps with a flashlight, a nightlight plugged into the wall, and his favorite blanket.

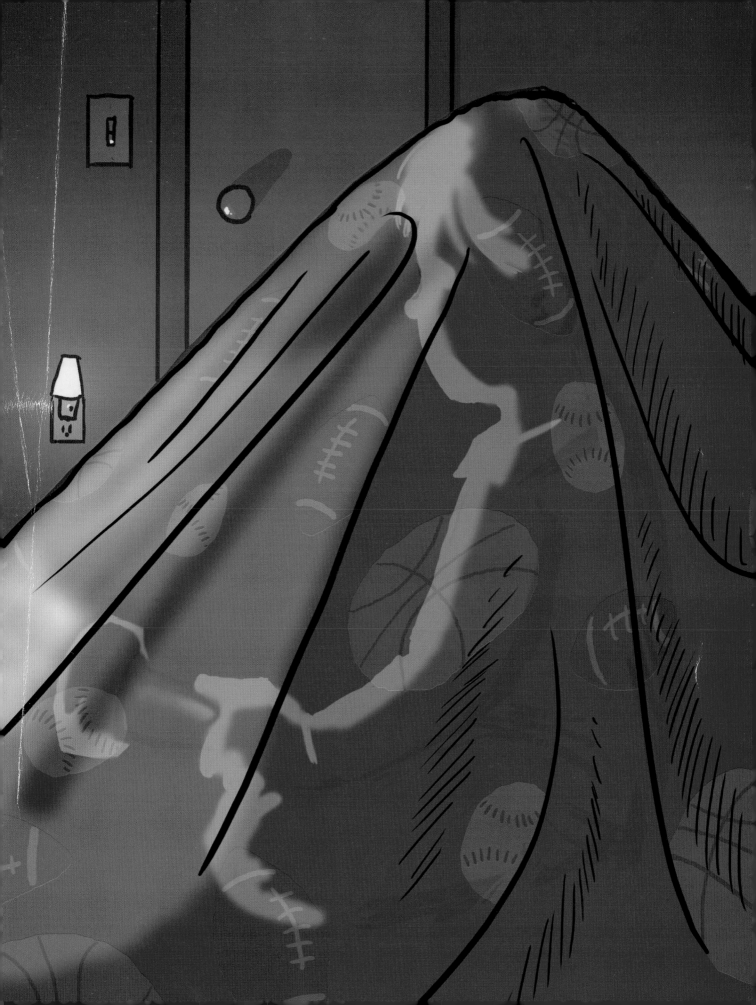

Sometimes Ben thinks
he hears noises at night.
When this happens, Ben
becomes very scared.
His parents tell him
that the noises are the
crickets and owl outside.

Ben still believes the
noises are from the
monsters under his bed
and in his closet.

When daylight breaks, Ben wakes up and is so happy to see the sun shining. It is time to eat breakfast and go outside to play.

Ben loves to play fetch with his dog.

Ben's parents call out to him and give him a present. It is a funny-looking little creature with an orange body, green swirls on its belly and back, and a big smile.

Mommy tells him that the creature is named Zimbobo.

Zimbobo is Ben's new protector from monsters.

Zimbobo has never been afraid of monsters. Zimbobo's special power is sending out ultrasonic waves that scare monsters away.

All Ben has to do is place Zimbobo anywhere he believes there are monsters. Zimbobo will keep him safe from all the bad monsters, and he will be saying "Goodbye, Monsters" in no time!

Ben is so excited! That evening, Ben places Zimbobo in his closet. As he crawls into bed, he wonders if he can finally say goodbye to the monsters that scare him.

All of a sudden, Ben wakes up. It is daylight. He made it through the night with no sign of any scary monsters!

"I made it through the night with no monsters!" Ben says proudly.

"Oh no!" Ben shouts. He made it through the night, but what about Zimbobo? Did Zimbobo make it through the night with the monsters in the closet? Ben runs to the closet and slowly opens the door.

To Ben's surprise, Zimbobo is safe and sound in the closet! Zimbobo's ultrasonic waves scared all of the monsters away.

Ben hugs and thanks Zimbobo for keeping him safe and finally helping him say goodbye to the monsters that scared him so much.

Now hurry up and don't delay. Zimbobo has arrived to make your fear of monsters go away!

Place Zimbobo in the scariest place.

You'll wake up saying "Goodbye, Monsters" with a smile on your face.